Name: _______________________________

Surname: _______________________________

Age: _______________________________

LET'S LEARN IN
A FUN
WAY

Here is your space, it's time to get creative

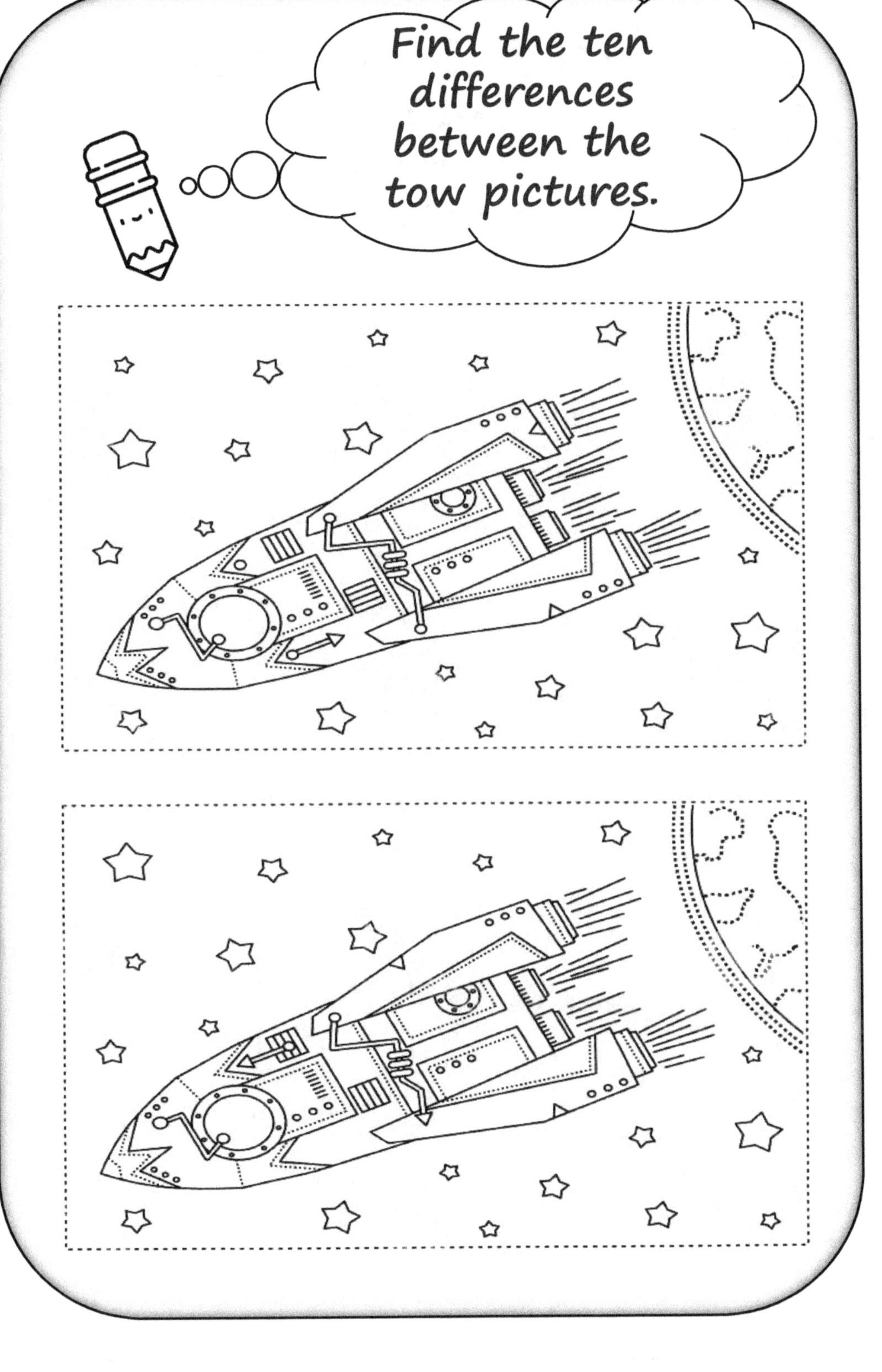

Find the ten
differences
between the
tow pictures.

Here is your space, it's time to get creative

Help cosmonaut
find path to
rocket

Here is your space,
it's time to get
creative

Football / Soccer

C	H	G	O	A	L	K	A	C	E
A	C	R	E	P	E	E	R	W	E
P	T	L	E	R	H	T	D	O	R
T	A	P	A	O	W	I	N	L	E
A	M	E	G	T	E	R	E	L	F
I	N	N	U	D	A	M	D	E	E
T	L	A	E	E	F	E	N	Y	R
Y	T	R	I	K	E	R	K	I	T
D	S	G	N	I	M	I	D	F	I
R	I	B	B	B	L	R	E	D	L	E

Find all the words from the word list
(ignore spaces and dashes):

CAPTAIN	MIDFIELDER
DEFENDER	PENALTY
DRIBBLING	REFEREE
GOALKEEPER	STRIKER
KIT	TEAM
LEAGUE	THROW-IN
MATCH	YELLOW CARD

Here is your space, it's time to get creative

Let's complete
the drawing
and color it.

Here is your space,
it's time to get
creative

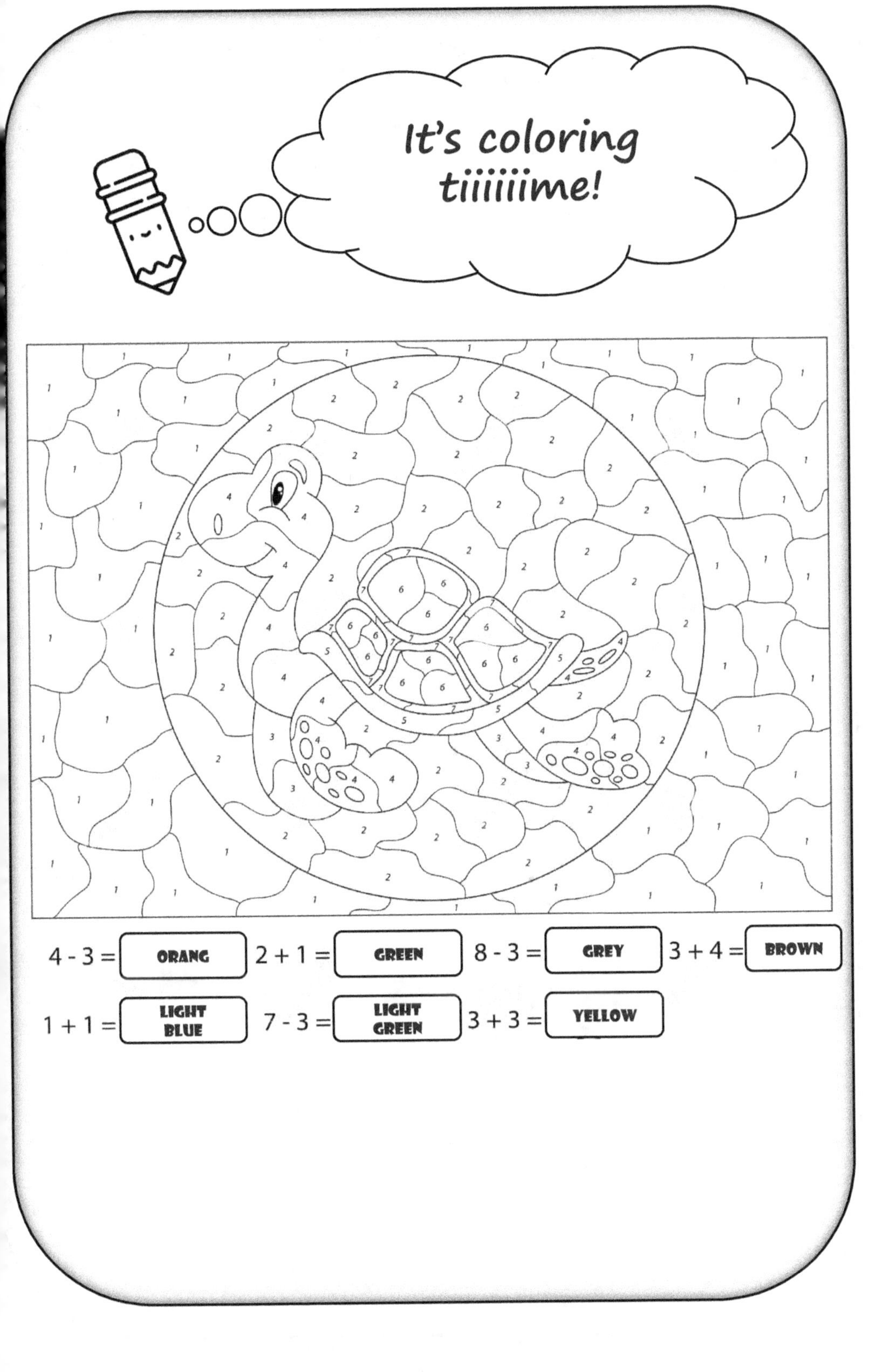

It's coloring tiiiiiime!
4 - 3 = ORANG
2 + 1 = GREEN
8 - 3 = GREY
3 + 4 = BROWN
1 + 1 = LIGHT BLUE
7 - 3 = LIGHT GREEN
3 + 3 = YELLOW

Here is your space, it's time to get creative

Can you help
the butterfly
to escape?

Here is your space,
it's time to get
creative

Find the two
identical
images.

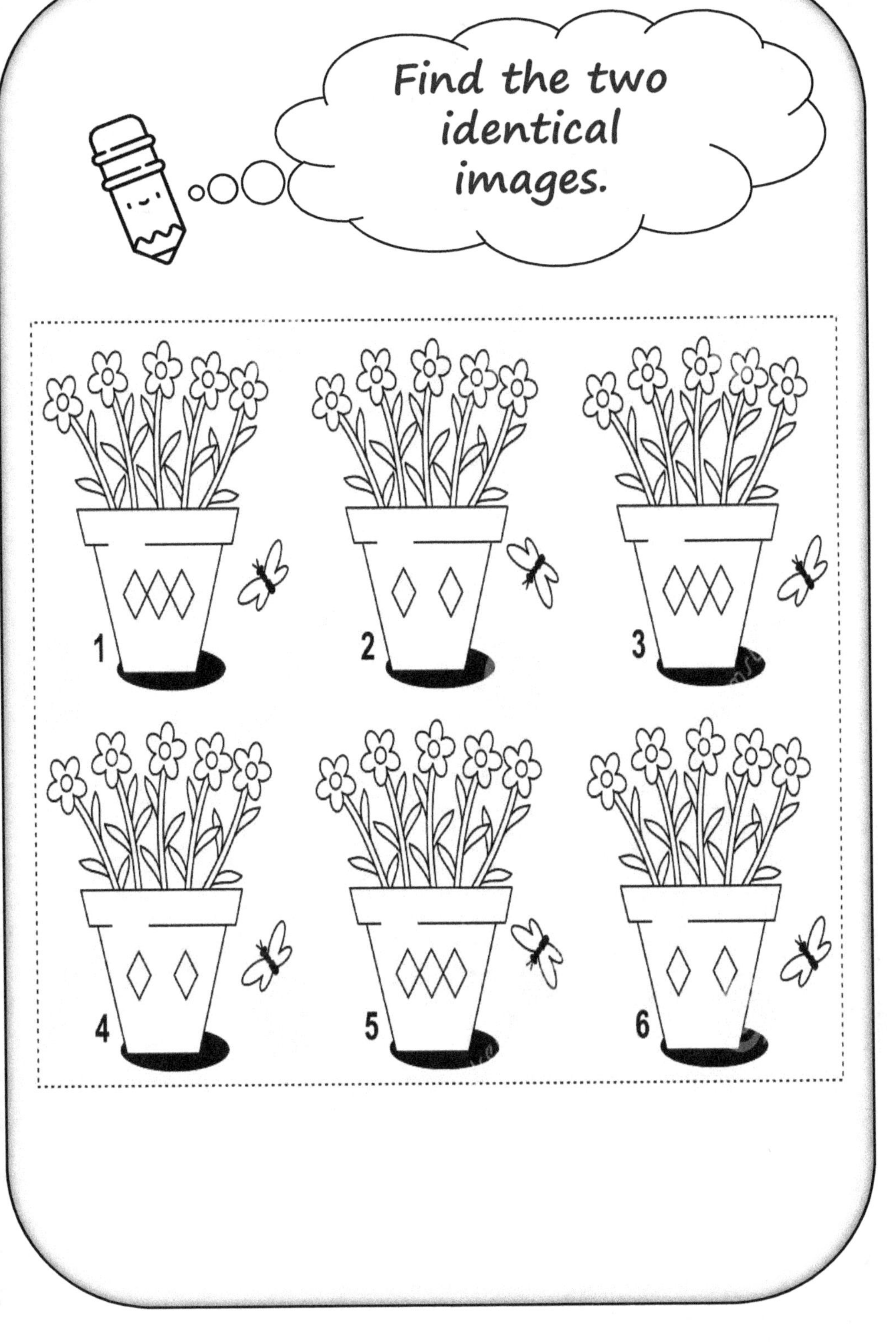

1
2
3
4
5
6

Here is your space,
it's time to get
creative

Musical Instruments

H	O	R	D	E	V	I	O	L	I
C	F	L	U	T	H	A	R	P	N
I	C	A	X	T	R	O	M	R	U
S	L	S	O	U	I	T	B	D	M
P	A	T	P	G	T	R	O	N	E
R	R	E	H	R	A	U	O	B	O
A	I	N	O	N	E	M	P	C	E
H	U	B	A	T	E	P	I	E	O
A	T	N	O	I	O	N	A	L	L
C	C	O	R	D	N	A	G	R	O

Find all the words from the word list
(ignore spaces and dashes):

ACCORDION

OBOE

CELLO

ORGAN

CLARINET

PIANO

DRUM

SAXOPHONE

FLUTE

TROMBONE

GUITAR

TRUMPET

HARP

TUBA

HARPSICHORD

VIOLIN

Here is your space, it's time to get creative

Let's complete
the drawing
and color it.

Here is your space,
it's time to get
creative

$3 \times 2 =$	YELLOW	$6 \times 2 =$	LIGHT YELLOW	$2 \times 8 =$	BROWN	$4 \times 6 =$	LIGHT GREEN	$4 \times 2 =$	GREY
$7 \times 2 =$	ORANGE	$2 \times 5 =$	WHITE	$5 \times 3 =$	LIGHT BLUE	$4 \times 5 =$	GREEN	$6 \times 3 =$	YELLOW

Here is your space,
it's time to get
creative

Help the
princess to go
to the palace.

Here is your space,
it's time to get
creative

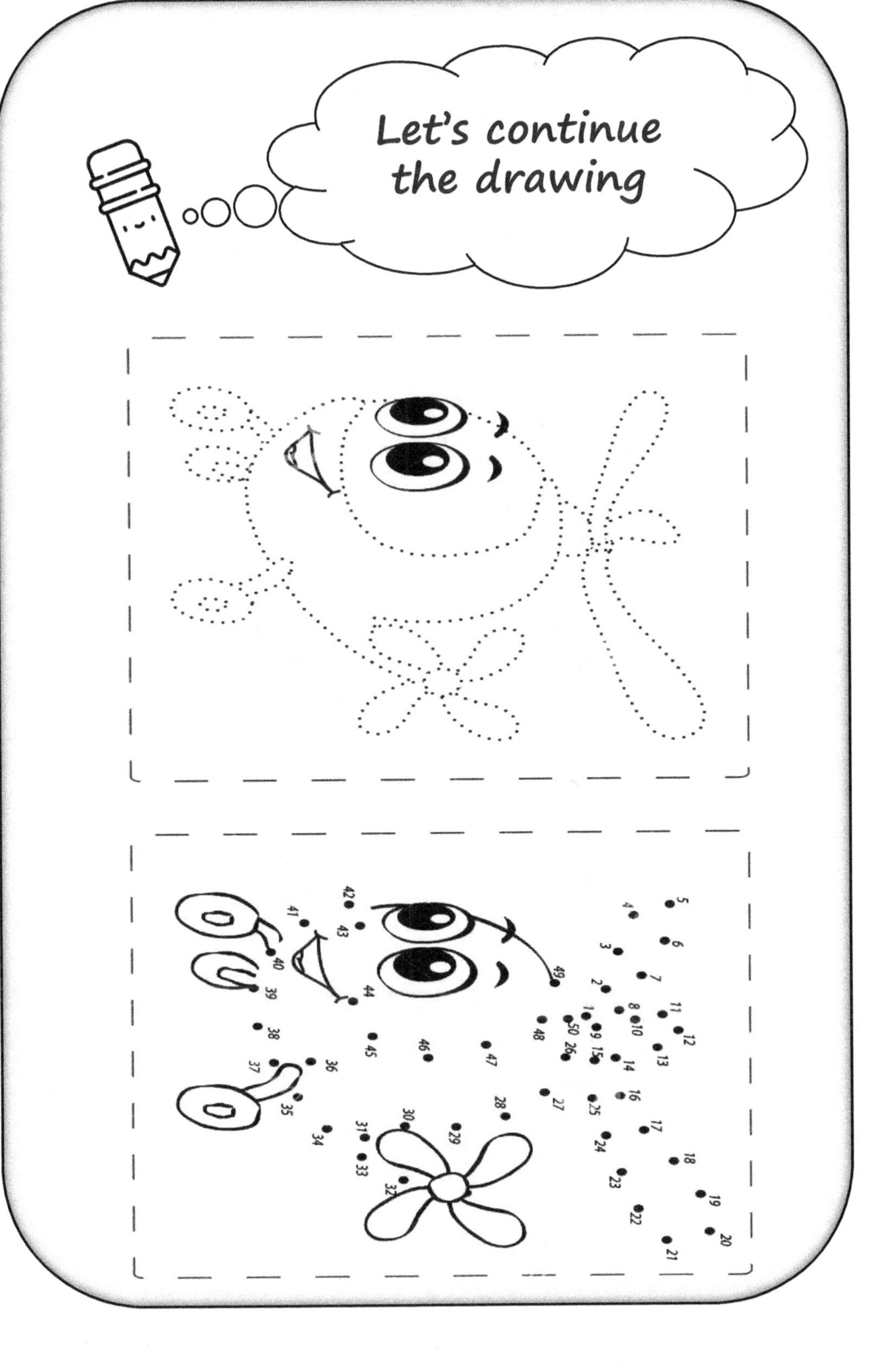
Let's continue
the drawing

Here is your space,
it's time to get
creative

Can you help
the hedgehog to
find the food?

Here is your space,
it's time to get
creative

Wild Cats

C	O	L	O	S	E	R	O	T	K
O	L	O	C	L	A	V	C	O	O
C	T	I	O	U	M	A	E	L	D
H	H	G	N	P	O	N	D	O	K
E	A	E	C	L	I	C	L	Y	N
E	T	R	I	A	L	A	N	U	X
M	A	R	L	L	A	R	A	L	L
Y	A	G	J	R	C	A	M	D	E
B	O	B	A	A	R	A	G	R	O
C	A	T	G	U	C	O	U	A	P

Find all the words from the word list
(ignore spaces and dashes, if any):

BOBCAT

CARACAL

CHEETAH

COLOCOLO

COUGAR

JAGUAR

KODKOD

LEOPARD

LION

LYNX

MANUL

MARGAY

OCELOT

ONCILLA

PUMA

SERVAL

TIGER

Here is your space,
it's time to get
creative

Let's complete
the drawing
and color it

Here is your space,
it's time to get
creative

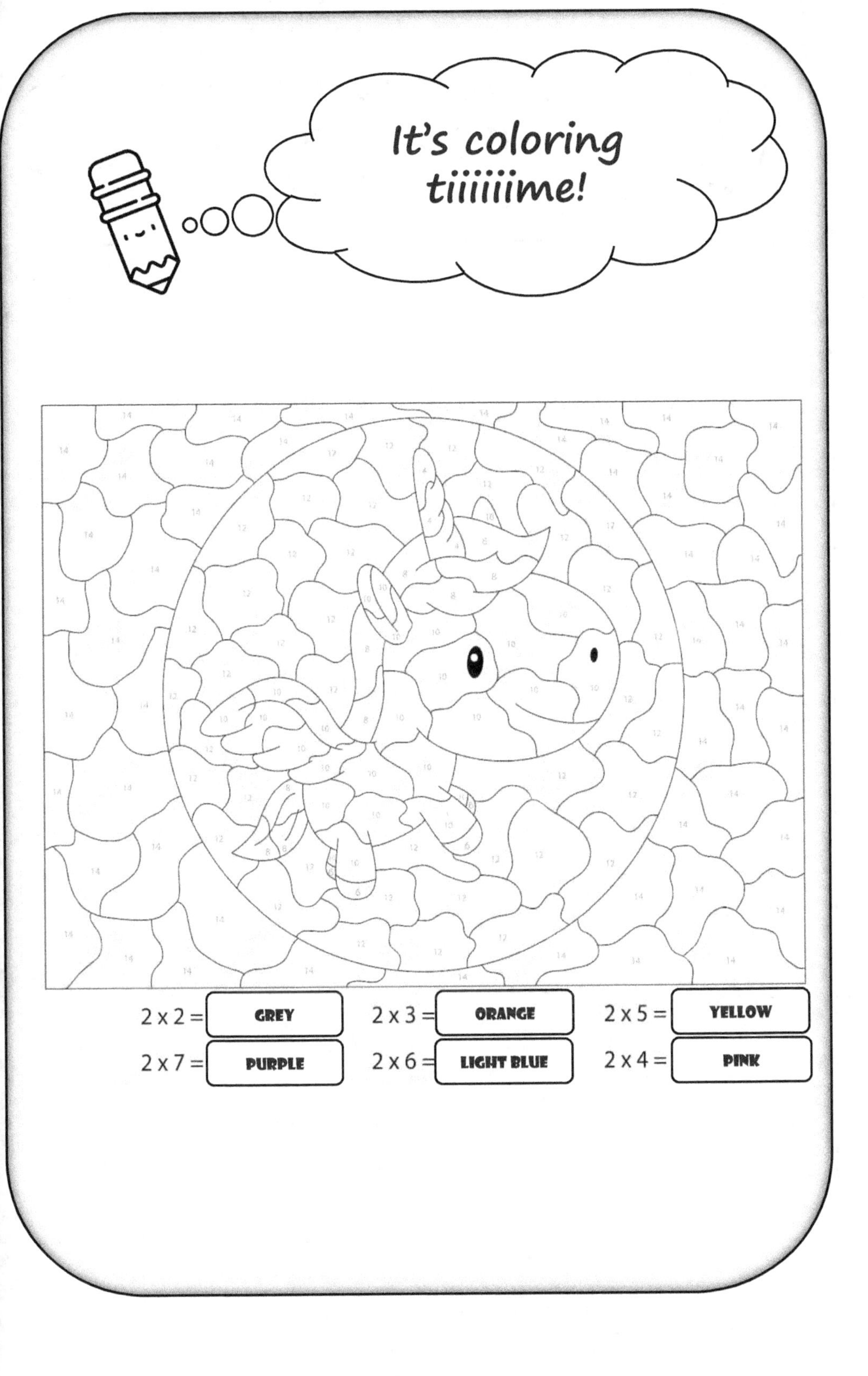

It's coloring
tiiiiiime!

2 x 2 =   GREY   2 x 3 =   ORANGE   2 x 5 =   YELLOW

2 x 7 =   PURPLE   2 x 6 =   LIGHT BLUE   2 x 4 =   PINK

Here is your space,
it's time to get
creative

Let's go through the maze.

Here is your space,
it's time to get
creative

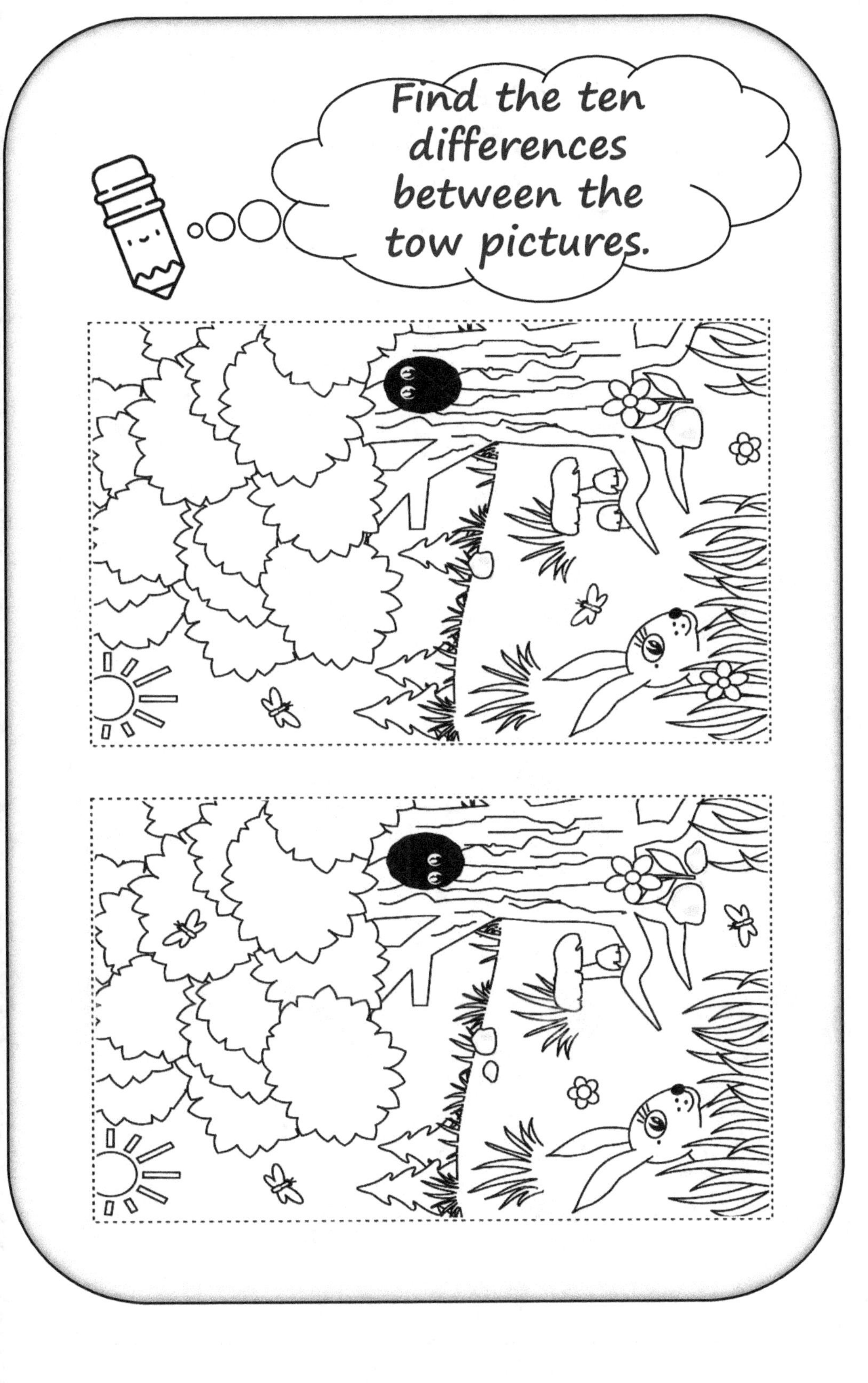

Find the ten
differences
between the
tow pictures.

Here is your space,
it's time to get
creative

Fruit and Berry

R	A	S	P	B	A	P	R	C	R
M	Y	R	R	E	P	L	I	H	A
A	O	E	P	A	P	U	C	E	E
N	G	A	C	H	P	M	O	R	P
O	E	U	L	B	L	E	T	R	Y
R	B	E	R	R	Y	P	I	N	E
A	E	B	A	N	E	L	P	P	A
N	G	A	N	A	N	O	L	E	M
T	I	U	R	F	W	A	T	E	R
G	R	A	P	E	N	O	M	E	L

Find all the words from the word list
(ignore spaces and dashes, if any):

APPLE
APRICOT
BANANA
BLUEBERRY
CHERRY
GRAPEFRUIT
LEMON
MANGO
ORANGE
PEACH

PEAR
PINEAPPLE
PLUM
RASPBERRY
WATERMELON

Here is your space,
it's time to get
creative

Do you know
the way to
treasure?

Here is your space, it's time to get creative

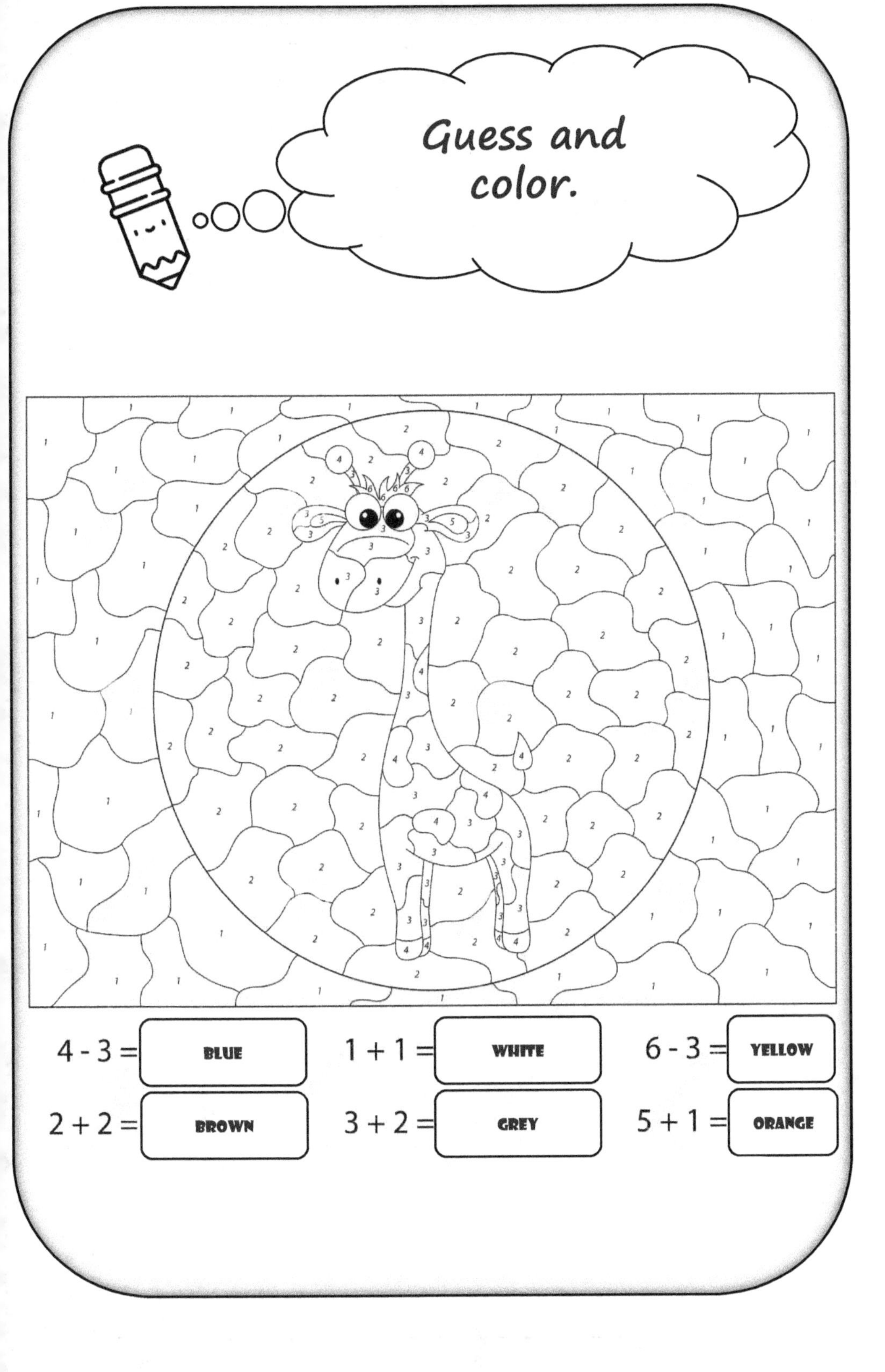
Guess and
color.
4 - 3 =   BLUE
2 + 2 =   BROWN
1 + 1 =   WHITE
3 + 2 =   GREY
6 - 3 =   YELLOW
5 + 1 =   ORANGE

Here is your space,
it's time to get
creative

Let's complete
the drawing
and color it.

Here is your space,
it's time to get
creative

Find the ten
differences
between the
tow pictures.

Here is your space,
it's time to get
creative

Solar System

P	L	A	O	I	D	B	E	L	T
T	E	N	R	L	U	T	O	J	U
A	S	T	E	P	C	O	R	E	P
M	O	O	N	E	A	M	S	T	I
S	U	N	S	N	R	E	T	M	G
V	U	T	P	E	T	H	Y	E	R
E	N	E	T	U	R	N	R	R	A
N	U	S	A	N	U	S	U	C	V
O	S	U	R	A	M	A	R	S	I
R	B	I	T	N	O	I	T	A	T

Find all the words from the word list
(ignore spaces and dashes):

ASTEROID BELT	NEPTUNE
COMETS	ORBIT
EARTH	PLANET
GRAVITATION	PLUTO
JUPITER	SATURN
MARS	SUN
MERCURY	URANUS
MOONS	VENUS

Here is your space,
it's time to get
creative

Let's complete
the drawing.

Here is your space,
it's time to get
creative

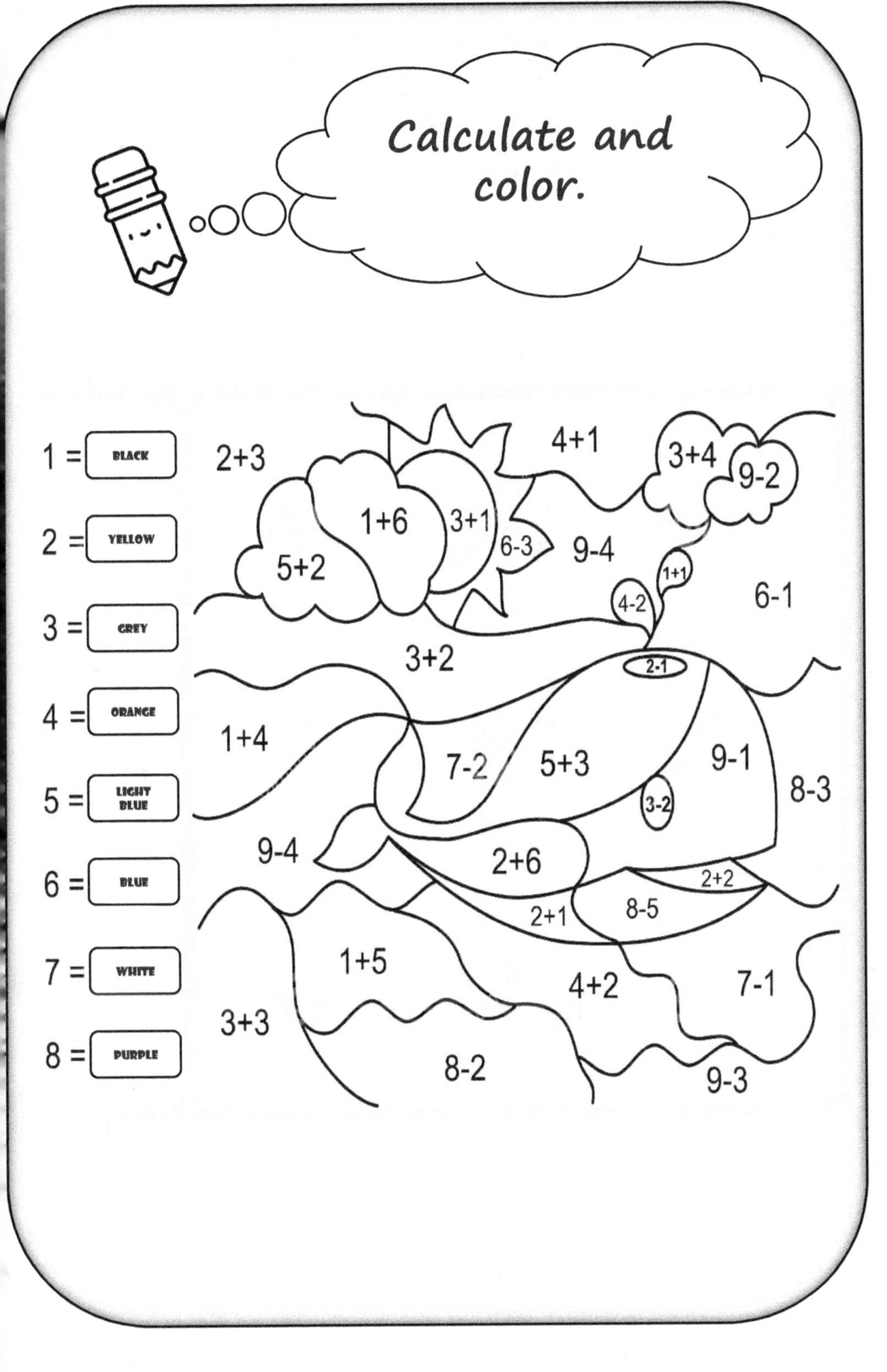

Calculate and color.

1 = BLACK
2 = YELLOW
3 = GREY
4 = ORANGE
5 = LIGHT BLUE
6 = BLUE
7 = WHITE
8 = PURPLE

2+3
1+6
3+1
5+2
6-3
4+1
3+4
9-2
9-4
1+1
4-2
6-1
3+2
2-1
1+4
7-2
5+3
9-1
8-3
3-2
9-4
2+6
2+2
2+1
8-5
1+5
4+2
7-1
3+3
8-2
9-3

Here is your space, it's time to get creative